Contents

Copyright

Character Profiles:

Kenzo Ogushi:

Description: Kenzo Ogushi is the protagonist of the story, a skilled and determined young warrior with silver hair, inherited from his Ogushi bloodline. He carries the burden of avenging his fallen clan and protecting the Musenge Bloodline. Throughout the story, Kenzo evolves from a lone survivor to seeking vengeance

Personality: Brave, determined, and compassionate. He is fiercely protective of his friends and family, always putting their safety before his own.

Danzai Musenge:

Description: Danzai is the leader of the Musenge Bloodline, a powerful warrior with lightning abilities passed down through generations. He initially has reservations about Kenzo but grows to respect and trust him during their journey together.

Personality: Wise, loyal, and courageous. He values the unity of his people and will do whatever it takes to protect them.

Yoshida:

Description: Yoshida was a messenger who served the Ogushi Clan and later fought alongside Kenzo and Danzai. He becomes a close friend and ally to both, proving his worth as a skilled combatant. Yoshida's loyalty and bravery remains

Personality: Loyal, dedicated, and selfless. Yoshida is determined to fulfil his duty and protect those he cares about, even at great personal risk.

Lei Sasaki:

Description: Lei Sasaki is the main antagonist, a sadistic and power-hungry leader of the Sasaki Empire. He seeks to eliminate the Ogushi and Musenge Bloodlines to solidify his empire's dominance.

Personality: Ruthless, cunning, and arrogant. Lei believes in his invincibility and enjoys tormenting his enemies.

Alina Sasaki:

Description: Alina is Lei's loyal and equally sadistic ally. Alina relishes in causing pain and chaos, revelling in her role as Lei's enforcer.

Personality: Cruel, cunning, and relentless. Alina enjoys the thrill of battle and takes pleasure in inflicting suffering on her enemies.

Lana:

Description: Lana is a young woman who becomes a significant figure in Kenzo's life. Their connection deepens as they share their struggles and dreams. Despite not being a warrior like the others, Lana displays strength in her way.

Personality: Kind, compassionate, and supportive

Musenge Bloodline Soldiers:

Description: The brave warriors of the Musenge Bloodline fight alongside Danzai to protect their people and oppose the Sasaki Empire. They share a strong bond, viewing each other as family and fighting as a united force.

Personality: Fierce, loyal, and disciplined. The Musenge Bloodline soldiers are unwavering in their dedication to their leader and cause.

Sasaki Empire Soldiers:

Description: The soldiers of the Sasaki Empire, led by Lei and Alina. Initially driven by fear and loyalty to their tyrannical ruler, some of them begin to question their allegiance as the story unfolds.

Personality: Fearful, obedient, and ruthless. The Sasaki Empire soldiers are driven by the desire to maintain power and please their leader.

Acknowledgement

Hello, my supporters, I would look like to thank you my friends and family for being part of this journey of mine creating Kenzo's Legacy. thank you for being a constant source of inspiration. Your enthusiasm and passion for the subjects explored in this book have ignited my curiosity and drive.

About The Book

When my first book on Wattpad failed to gain the traction, I had envisioned being Samurai Ken, I initially felt disheartened. After releasing my second book I came back to the story it wouldn't be called Samurai Ken I would change the title to Kenzo's Legacy and completely change the plot of the story, but I keep some of the character's names from Samurai Ken.

Epigraph

You can't expect something to happen when you don't even try to take Action

Jonathan Slater

Prologue

In the land of Sasaki, where bloodlines held ancient power and legends were forged, darkness loomed, threatening to engulf everything in its path. For centuries, the Sasaki Empire had reigned with an iron fist, led by the ruthless Emperor Lei. His thirst for power knew no bounds, and he sought to crush any bloodline that dared to challenge his rule.

Amidst the chaos and oppression, a glimmer of hope emerged. The Ogushi Bloodline, once revered for its strength and valour, faced annihilation. However, a determined survivor, Kenzo, stood as the last descendant, clinging to a promise made long ago.

With the fate of his bloodline resting on his shoulders, Kenzo embarked on a journey, alongside his loyal friend and messenger, Yoshida, and an unlikely ally, Danzai. United by loss and a desire for justice, they set out to confront the mighty Sasaki Empire, even as their wounds from the past threatened to pull them apart.

Unbeknownst to them, their path was destined to be fraught with sacrifices, choices, and a legacy that would shape the course of history. As their destinies intertwined, an epic battle for redemption, freedom, and the survival of bloodlines began.

Chapter 1: Legacy of Kenzo

The Year 1865

The time of the samurai where chaos is a regular occurrence. But that will soon change as the story goes through the life of Kenzo

Kenzo is the man of a prophecy who has yet to find out who he is. Kenzo was brown skin, white hair like the clouded sky and possessed the physic of a professional athlete. The twenty-one-year-old was raised in a village called Nuville where he learns to appreciate and cherish the people around him. He stayed on the outskirts of the world being on the more poverty side of the world where crime rates were slightly higher.

Morning

Kenzo in his village was loved by everyone as If he was the people's saviour in Nuville, wearing his blue kimono shining more than everyone else as he stands out the most.

He goes to buy some stuff from the market when a group of bandits approached him with the bandits wielding nasty, dusty weapons.

"Give us everything that you have!" growled the leader of the bandits, who was tall and well-built, Kenzo immediately knew this was a bad situation. His eyes darted around, looking for a way to avoid confrontation.

"I don't have anything to give," said Kenzo trying to sound as brave as possible. It was a lie, Kenzo thought that giving away his money would only influence the bandits even more to commit more threats, so he decided to neglect them.

"You sure you want to do this?" the bandit leader said glaring at Kenzo.

"It's exactly what I want to do," Kenzo said as he fires back at the bandit leader.

Kenzo sensed a fight about to break down, there were rare times when Kenzo had to get into a physical fight. The ones that trained him to defend himself were no other than his fellow villagers. The bandit leader charged at Kenzo with his swinging sword. Kenzo dodged the first strike and kneed the bandit leader in the abdomen.

The bandit leader was in agony, which initiated the rest of the bandits to attack Kenzo, but Kenzo manhandled every one of them, displaying art to the ones watching. All the bandits were knocked out first flat on the ground.

"I advise you not to try that again with me or anyone else, do you understand me?" Kenzo said sternly

"The bandits mumbled saying 'yes'. The atmosphere changed once Kenzo defeated the bandits.

The villagers thanked him and continued with their day. "Now that is sorted, time to buy some food," Kenzo said eagerly

As he explores the food market, He doesn't know a mysterious figure is watching him from the background.

Kenzo opens the door to his small home and turns on his light, where his heartbeat increased as the mysterious figure stood in his home like a statue. Before Kenzo can say anything, the mysterious person momentarily covered his mouth preventing him from speaking, The person had a male voice as he whispered, "Be quiet".

The person took down their hand and the robe. The man had parted black shiny hair, was aged 40s, wearing a purple tactical outfit. He looked at Kenzo as if he was something he's been searching for his whole life.

"Who are you?" Kenzo said

"My name is Yoshida; I am a former messenger also the one that brought you here in Nuville," Yoshida said

Kenzo was confused as everything that was happening in the morning went from zero to a hundred.

"I know it's weird, but there's a lot of things that you don't know about, that includes yourself," Yoshida said.

"What do you mean about me?" Kenzo was lost for words on what Yoshida's point was.

Yoshida gently gets on his knees getting Kenzo even more baffled. "Lord Kenzo Ogushi, it is time for you to fulfil your legacy," Yoshida spoke like a disciple

Once Kenzo heard the word Ogushi, legacy and master, his curiosity reached a high level as it reminded him that he has no memory of having parents let alone knowing their names.

Kenzo always thought he would live a normal life, but he was wrong.

"Lord Kenzo Ogushi I want you to step out these doors and say one word to the villagers... Ogushi." Yoshida politely asked

"I need answers from you first!" Kenzo desperately said but Yoshida told him to "just do what I tell you."

∗∗∗

He stepped outside once again looking around the village preparing to say the word: "OGUSHI!"

Everyone stopped what they were doing and looked at Kenzo for a moment until they all bowed to him responding "OGUSHI GREAT ONE!"

Yoshida stepped outside to see Kenzo's reaction, what he saw was a young man who realized that there was more to him than he thought.

"The time has finally come"-Villager

"We raised him for twenty-one years now it's the moment he learns about his legacy."-Villager 2

"Guys, what is going on, why're you all bowing to me? Please stop." Kenzo said

Kenzo wished all of these were a dream, but it was real life.

"Kenzo, you're not dreaming," said Yoshida whilst he tries to reason with Kenzo. Kenzo tried to punch Yoshida only for Yoshida to grab onto his hand.

"Who I am?" Kenzo said subtlety

"You're the present! If you want to know more about yourself gradually, follow me as I

will teach you the way of the samurai"
Yoshida said

It took a minute for Kenzo to listen to take in what Yoshida said but went with him. As he looks back following Yoshida to the outskirts of the village, he sees the villagers in tears, Kenzo wondered why but there was too much occurring early in the day that he couldn't ask "Why are you crying?"

***

The sun was setting as the two arrived at the outskirts side of the village where Yoshida crafted two wooden swords giving one to Kenzo. "What Is this for," Kenzo said

"This my lord is for your training."-Yoshida said warming up

"Training right now."-Kenzo

"Yes, right now."-Yoshida

Yoshida was standing fighting position ready to strike Kenzo. "Don't lie to me when I ask you this, when you were younger used to do a little sword practice with you?"

The more Yoshida spoke to Kenzo about his past years, the more Kenzo thought Yoshida was a creep.

"How do you know all of this?" Kenzo rubs his head

"Don't forget I am the one who brought you to Nuville when you were born to add to that I am the one who gave instructions to the villagers on how to take of you as well.

Kenzo was in utter disbelief. "You see Kenzo there's one thing that you need to understand about yourself that you're not ordinary, you're a special boy… part of the Ogushi bloodline who are as most would say the chosen ones. The masters of the sword. It may be a lot for you to understand but soon enough everything will come full circle." Yoshida spoke in the sincerest way

Kenzo had an idea

"I'll tell you what I'll fight against you Yoshida and you have to leave if I win." Kenzo boldly challenged Yoshida

"Pointless challenge but I accept, if I win you will train and fulfil your legacy." Yoshida chuckles

Kenzo was in a fighting position to start his duel with Yoshida. Yoshida told him to 'come'. Kenzo rushed at Yoshida clashing with their wooden swords, Immediately Kenzo was trying to land some offence on Yoshida.

For Yoshida, he did not need to hit back against Kenzo; it was like fighting an undeveloped child that couldn't function right. Kenzo slowly boosted his attack speed like turning up the level of a treadmill.

Yoshida yawns irritating Kenzo to even go quicker with his attacks nevertheless struggled to the point that Yoshida was mocking Kenzo. Yoshida swept Kenzo and struck him at the same time knocking Kenzo out clean.

"I guess I win."

The next day In Nuville, Kenzo wakes up in his house. "That was a weird dream" Kenzo was feeling relaxed.

"As I say again, it's not a dream" Yoshida standing inside Kenzo's house which makes Kenzo scream humorously.

"Come on training now." Yoshida steps outside.

The duo goes back to the same spot where Kenzo suffered defeat in a humiliating fashion. The first thing they did was go for long runs around the area. Yoshida incorporated strength, speed, agility, balance and flexibility in Kenzo's training using any useful material, everything was going well until it came to the basics of using a samurai sword. Kenzo struggles to understand the power within him and his training went on for two weeks.

At midnight, Kenzo was sleeping when he starts to have visions that weren't clear to him, when he woke up, his body felt completely different as if something was hugging him.

✳✳✳

It was sunset again, the wind breathing out the leaves into the high sky. Yoshida was sitting down meditating as he waits for Kenzo. He senses his presence opens his eyes and sees Kenzo standing before him but this time, there was total concentration coming from the young one.

"I feel a little different from the master now," Yoshida said to himself.

"I'm ready," Kenzo said in significance. He steps forward, blinks his eyes in an instant and eyes started to shine white which Yoshida notices and stands up.

Yoshida felt joy.

The two squared off again with victory already being in his favour. Yoshida remained calm and collected against Kenzo but none of his strikes landed on him thanks to Kenzo's lightning-quick reflexes allowing him to strike back with equal force he suffered the past days. The two were now fighting like equals as they verse each other, but victory fell into the hands of Kenzo barely earning the victory.

Yoshida was a happy man as Kenzo maybe be able to travel with him now. "Let me help you up" Kenzo lifts Yoshida back to his feet. They stare at each other having an intuition this could be a long-term friendship.

"Are you ready for your legacy, Master Kenzo?"

"I am ready, but first I want to say something to my family."

***

Kenzo called all the villagers saying one message before he goes with Yoshida.

"It seems everyone has known everything about me. My blood parents and bloodline and all sort of stuff. Despite you guys having the knowledge to tell me everything right now but I have decided to choose that I'm going to find out everything for myself.

Everyone in the village wished him good luck in his adventures as he said, "He will be back."

Kenzo says goodbye.

∗∗∗

As the two are walking, Yoshida tells Kenzo he needs to collect something, when he comes back it a weapon being a bow and arrow.

"What's that for?" Kenzo said

"This Master Kenzo is the actual weapon that I use, I'm not a swordsman, what I was teaching you was a bit more of the basics"- Yoshida said

"So, what about me I'm only stuck with a wooden sword. When do I get a real one?" Kenzo said in desperation. Yoshida put his hand on Kenzo's shoulder saying "The time will come"

They set off to fulfil the legacy.

***

The day became night, bats flying across the sky. Red lights flash everywhere from an Empire like a lighthouse. The city was called the Sasaki Empire packed with so many people that from a massive view they looked like microscopes. Guards wearing their armour were guarding a specific dojo.

***

Inside the dojo a man sitting on a throne had people worshipping him, for him, it was respect on the other hand the worshippers inside felt nothing but terror. The worshippers repeated saying "Lord Lei Sasaki"

Lei was built-like one in a thousand, Asian man with elderly hair. He wore a red kimono with a black robe behind them. The man was as ferocious as a great white shark displaying happy emotion. Within him lay a dark history

Who is this man?

Chapter 2: Danzai Musenge

Tuesday Afternoon

Yoshida and Kenzo were now travelling together to deliver the conquest of Kenzo's legacy. It was Kenzo's first time travelling because he has spent twenty-one years of his life in Nuville, Kenzo felt happiness being able to explore the rest of the world as he can experience landmarks, clothing, food and lots of other stuff. "Man, this is going to be awesome." Said Kenzo. "It sure is" Yoshida responded.

Yoshida wanted to collect equipment for their travels for daily things an average human would do. Later the two sat down on a log, he wanted to speak to Kenzo about a very cunning samurai and ruler. "Master Kenzo, for you to obtain your legacy there are two people you must defeat to achieve it, these two people being part of the Sasaki bloodline… a female name Alina Sasaki nicknamed the ruthless one that serves the ruler and number one of all bloodlines…Lei Sasaki" Yoshida said superficially.

"Alina and Lei Sasaki?" Kenzo said

"Yes, those two have dominated the world for the past twenty-one years … They're the ones responsible for your parent's death," Yoshida said

Lei and Alina know nothing of Kenzo's existence also being the last one of the Ogushi bloodline.

"When it comes to the bloodline that I am part of what exactly happened to my bloodline?" asked Kenzo. Yoshida told them "They all died by the Sasaki blades but most of the death happened at the hands of Lei and Alina themselves. The problem with the Sasaki's is they're able to manipulate blood within their bodies no matter what type of blood it is enhancing their natural abilities with their blades and allowing them to perform outrageous techniques." Yoshida carefully explained to Kenzo.

"So, there are only two bloodlines?" Kenzo said

"There's one more… the Musenge bloodline"- Yoshida told Kenzo

"Musenge bloodline?"

"The Musenge bloodline you can say is the weakest out of the three but not by far as they're able to have efficient use of lighting. The bloodline represents themselves wearing a black kimono with a white dragon emblem behind their back." Yoshida said.

"So, what happened to that bloodline?" Kenzo was intrigued by the story. "Rumour has it that there's only a small group of them left that managed to survive the Sasaki invasions. That's what I heard from the past years but I haven't seen any yet.

"I see" Kenzo rubs his head

"You never know we might be lucky to even find someone part of the Musenge bloodline someday," Yoshida said as he stood up from the log.

The two were walking through a forest when foes appeared right before their eyes. The foes wore red armour with blood symbols "Just when we were talking about them this has to happen" Yoshida sighs

"What who are they?" Kenzo asked in worry

"The red armour should be enough for you to figure out who they're… Idiots of the Sasaki bloodline army" Yoshida said in disgust.

"Really?"

The Sasaki soldiers instantly recognised who Yoshida was but had no clue who was with him. "Well, well look who it is boys Yoshida the messenger who served the ruler of the Ogushi and now you appear once again just for you to die by the hands of the Sasaki blood including this boy with you."

The Sasaki soldiers unleashed their bloodline power but to their surprise, their opponents vanished but appeared again with their quick dodging skills with Kenzo using his wooden sword and Yoshida using his custom bow and arrow. The Sasaki soldier's underestimation caused them a beating "I was taught one thing where I am from, never lowball your opponent."

Yoshida and Kenzo obliterate their opponents but shortly after the Sasaki soldiers stood back turning the tables on the two as the soldiers took them more seriously.

"Wow, you two had us for a second, it's tough it will put you to sleep permanently" the Sasaki soldiers grip their blades.

As the Sasaki soldiers are about to finish them off, lightning strikes them. They look to see what caused that when it was a light day, the soldiers looked behind seeing a swordsman wearing a black kimono with a white dragon emblem behind their back. The Group said, "NO WAY IT CAN'T BE A... MUSENGE".

The unknown swordsman stands facing the soldiers as he appeared as dark skin, small afro headed young man.

The first word he said was:

MUSENGE FLASHING LIGHT!

The swordsman steeped and as he stepped, he went through them in less than a second, leaving slashes everywhere on their body also destroying their armour completely. The Sasaki soldiers passed out on the ground.

The only ones standing were Keno, Yoshida and the Musenge swordsman that appeared before them. Keno and Yoshida did not believe what they witnessed.

"Who are you?" the Musenge swordsman asked Yoshida and Keno.

The swordsman helped them but didn't trust them at the same time.

"Listen we're not here trouble in a matter of fact you may want to be allied with us." Yoshida trying to negotiate with the swordsman.

"Why Is that," he asked

"Next to me is the last Ogushi," Yoshida said

Ignoring the fact, the swordsman says "Wait a minute, I have heard of you before no I have seen you before Yoshida, right? You're alive."

"Well, I just can't die," he said

"Listen we're both part of bloodlines can we just get along," Keno said as he tries to greet the Musenge swordsman, but the swordsman was sceptical of Kenzo, so he stepped back and positioned his sword.

"I'm not trying to fight you" Keno trying to step back

"I don't care," said the swordsman

Kenzo noticed that the Musenge swordsman wasn't being as aggressive as he was against the Sasaki soldiers, Keno quickly started to attack the Musenge swordsman as he refused to back down which made the swordsman acknowledge him a little.

What came next was soon as the swordsman is about to strike down Kenzo he looked into his eyes and started to see the past of Kenzo's birth and the power he will hold that can destroy the Sasaki bloodline for good. The Musenge Swordsman with his sword aimed at Kenzo froze like ice. "Hello," Kenzo repeated.

Yoshida realised what happened.

"There's no way, I thought the Ogushi were extinct but no… there is one left…you. I feel it now" The swordsman felt a surge of emotion boiling in his body to the point that the swordsman told Yoshida and Kenzo what his name is and put his hand in a handshake motion saying:

"My name is Danzai Musenge of the Musenge bloodline, it is an honour to meet you Ogushi One"

"Nice to meet you, Danzai of the Musenge bloodline."

There was no animosity between them once Danzai realised Kenzo was an Ogushi.

"You two come with me"- Danzai said

✳✳✳

The two were following Danzai until they stopped near a road confused about where Danzai was taking them, but they won't be any more when Danzai said "Musenge open" A part of the road opened like an underground square door. Under the square opening were other people that Yoshida and Kenzo couldn't see."

**

When the three entered through the underground square door, orange lights turned on and the figures that Yoshida and Kenzo couldn't see before their entered were the few Musenge bloodline members. Yoshida specifically was surprised by their survival.

The Musenge bloodline was not clear why Danzai brought two outsiders but just like Danzai it took time for them to figure out who Yoshida yet having no clue who Kenzo was. They show hostility towards him. Danzai tried to persuade them when he said, "Listen my blood, I have something to say that will give us the encouragement to go against Lei Sasaki, is this man right here" Danzai pointed out Kenzo

"Who is he?" One of the Musenge asked Danzai in caution.

Danzai laughed telling his blood to look into the eyes of Kenzo and in an instant they experienced the exact feeling Danzai did. Once that was over for them, there wasn't a single word said but dramatically the perspective of Kenzo changed for them.

"I'T CAN'T BE, AN OGUSHI RIGHT IN FRONT OF US!"

"You saw it didn't you"-Danzai said

"What are they seeing?" Kenzo asked Yoshida as he is watching the Musenge bloodline look at him with utter surprise.

"What they see is the past birth and the future proving that you're an Ogushi. I can't see because I'm not part of a bloodline... your father is the one that told me about this. Don't even ask what happens in the future either." Said Yoshida

"No fair" Kenzo said in displeasure

Two seconds after, the Musenge bloodline showed their respect for him. Kenzo went with the flow. 20 minutes later, Musenge bloodline sits down with Kenzo asking him what he has been doing his whole life so far, whether he knows who he is and how much potential is within him.

Kenzo couldn't answer all their questions but attempted the best he could.

When they were done, Yoshida, Kenzo and Danzai were having a discussion. "So how long has your bloodline been hiding?" Yoshida asked.

"We haven't been hiding for the entire time, for years we've been strategizing on how we could get rid of the Sasaki bloodline but no matter what we did, more of us would end up dying including my father. Guess who has done it?" Danzai asked Yoshida

"Lei" he answered but Danzai said "No, it was his right hand… Alina Sasaki who killed my father."

"Sorry for that said Yoshida and Kenzo

After that, all three men came to an agreement that they should team up.

"We shall bring peace to the world, first we would need to break past the Sasaki District" said Danzai. Yoshida had one thing to say before Danzai finished his sentence. "Sorry Danzai, there's somewhere I want to take Kenzo after we pull through Sasaki District, I want to take him to the Ogushi home. Danzai agreed to it.

Before they took off again with Danzai being involved in their journeys now, Danzai wanted to say something to his bloodline "I can't risk any more of you dying, so I'll be embarking with these two gentlemen to help get rid of Lei, Alina and the entire Sasaki bloodline, they've had their way long enough. Now the Ogushi blood standing beside me gives me a new level of resilience, everyone give me your courage!"

Everyone raised their swords in respect.

Stepping out once again, all three men allied to destroy their biggest enemy, Lei Sasaki.

Now they walk to the Sasaki District.

Chapter 3: The Sasaki Underground District

The Sasaki Empire

Lei in his structured dojo is fighting against his army without breaking a sweat, it was as if the man was not human at all. "We've been fighting for hours and we still can't touch him," One of the Sasaki soldiers said.

Lei was fighting his man like having a walk in the park while a Hispanic woman in her 40s, embodies a captivating blend of grace and strength. Her fit physique reflects her dedication to maintaining a healthy lifestyle. Draped in a vibrant red kimono, Alina exudes an air of elegance and confidence. Her choice of clothing adds a touch of cultural flair, showcasing her appreciation for tradition while embracing her unique style.

"So much noise in here"- The woman said

"We're in a dojo Alina you can't expect peace in here" said Lei as he continues to fight his men, after Lei carelessly humiliates his underlings, he walks off with Alina. He tells his men to "Get up and go home"

The two walk through the empire with people bowing to them, not looking up until they're completely out of their site.

Lei asked, "Alina I have a question for you, do you think anyone here respects me or is it just fear in disguise."

Alina answered his question saying, "If you want my honesty it is simply fear, to be honest, I thought you would have a feeling that no one respects me if you mind me saying."

"I have no problem with it, I appreciate

honesty," said Lei.

✳✳✳

In his sizable area, Lei was catching a rubdown like an emperor that committed to doing hours of service to the people. Lei's mind was wandering about something, an unknown figure that started to crawl on his head. "Alina we've been in control for twenty years and now all these years why I feel like… someone will strike down," Lei said

"I do not know how to answer that question for you, I'm afraid."

"That's a shame," he said

Standing on the top of the empire where they were watching everyone with their bloodlust eyes get on with their lives, Lei found it to be humorous while Alina saw things as nought.

It was them against the world.

"Power over others was fun in the first year we took over, but when I killed off Mahi things became boring. What can I do at the end of the day I decided to take out the strongest Ogushi, I was the only one capable of doing it now here we are glorifying in success" Lei said in happiness

"Yes… we are" Alina said

✳✳✳

The Next Day

"I never thought going somewhere would require so much walking, I hate it," said a restless Kenzo. The three went paused their journey and stopped by the tiny I'oland land where they can to a chance to get some food and water while trying to be as discrete as possible. They couldn't afford to stay for long as Danzai and Kenzo are now aware of how recognisable Yoshida is. Lucky for them there were no Sasaki bloodline members.

"So how far are we again from the Sasaki District?" Kenzo asked

"We are not far; you can say we are somewhat closing in but not at the same time," Danzai said

The three continue their long walks bypassing many roads until the day morphed into the night, someplace they stopped moving and hiding as the group saw civilians entering

Danzai and Yoshida said "This is the Sasaki District" as they saw Sasaki soldiers.

The three men knew it wouldn't be wise for them to just attack but fortunately for them, out of the Sasaki soldier's reach, they see three people getting the idea to take their clothes putting them to sleep pleasingly. They proceed to walk in the Sasaki District fooling the soldiers.

"Holy" Kenzo said as he, Yoshida and Danzai witnessed the spectacular District immune in luxurious material. It was anyone's dream to be in.

"This place is wonderful indeed, but it's in the hands of someone who doesn't deserve it," Yoshida said.

"Now, what is the next step?" Danzai asked Yoshida

"Well, the Sasaki exit leads to the Ogushi land then to the Sasaki empire straight ahead of us, I didn't put too much thought into this... not enough planning can lead to chaos" Yoshida said worrying.

While Yoshida and Danzai were discussing how they were going to execute getting to the other side of the Sasaki District, Kenzo had his eyes set on a woman. She moved gracefully through the people in the Sasaki District, her long brunette hair flowing like a river behind her. In the dim lights of the bright district, she seemed to glow, her skin was luminous and spotless.

Dressed in elegant silk robes and her eyes sparkled with a beauty that made Kenzo breathless.

As he watched, he felt nothing but sadness from her on the inside. Kenzo began to follow her without Danzai and Yoshida noticing until one minute later.

"Where did Kenzo go" They froze

As he follows the lady, he is unaware that the female can perceive his presence leading him to an ally and hitting him in his orchis.

"That hurts!" he said.

The woman looked at him menacingly responding "Why are you following me? you moron"

Kenzo had no experience with women, so he was clueless about how weird he looked. He was trying to focus on the mission, but he couldn't help himself acknowledge the female's beauty.

"Hello, can you hear me, why are you following me?" she said

Kenzo did not know how to handle this type of situation, he was lost about most things. "I'm sorry was I being weird," he said.

"You think, clearly to me you don't know a lot of stuff don't you, also how old are by the way?". Kenzo answered her saying "I am Twenty-One"

The woman found it a coincidence that Kenzo was the same age as her. Their interaction became even more uneasy when Kenzo straightforwardly asked her "I'm going to cut to the chase, you're very attractive and I think I like you" Kenzo said bravely.

The woman was caught off-guard that she could not help but unintentionally blush. She tried to run away but once again Kenzo chased after her. At the same time, Yoshida and Danzai were looking for Kenzo while maintaining their disguises.

"We must find him quick; I think he will stand out too much," Danzai said.

"I'll think. if there is one thing that leads him to get distracted."

They both grasped something and sighed in frustration.

"He is definitely with a female," They both said.

After running for such a long time, she stopped being out of breath. Kenzo asked what her name was.

She gave in telling Kenzo her name was "Lana, what's yours?"

"I am Kenzo," he said as he shakes her hand elegantly. Lana couldn't crack what Kenzo's intentions were however it wasn't halting her from hanging out with him even though she just met him.

The two seem to open up to each other in very little time with Lana telling how she has been raised in the Sasaki District learning nothing but being a slave to beauty saying, "I'm never going to experience the outside world and I will never will." Lana said

"It's never too late to experience something that you desire no matter if it takes days, weeks, months even over a year eventually what you want will come to you," Kenzo said inspiring Lana.

Yoshida and Danzai finally found Kenzo "We knew it" they both said.

Another thing occurred now. The whole time they thought they were in the clear was highly mistaken as they were being monitored this whole time.

"Crap we've been caught."

No questions, plans or anything, all three fighters defended themselves against anyone who tried to face them, shortly after Kenzo took Lana out of the danger zone then he jumps back into battle with Yoshida and Danzai. They were now drawing too much attention like a worldwide event. Lana as she was watching Kenzo fighting, thought Kenzo had something in him, she couldn't help but react to him.

"How many are coming?" Yoshida frustratedly said.

MUSENGE LIGHT STRIKE

Lighting poured from Danzai's blade as he became offensive to his opponent shocking everyone to oblivion what appeared before the group that looked like an entire army. Danzai wasn't fighting at his fullest worried about the many casualties he could cause to the innocent people.

"I see what's going on," Kenzo said to himself. He with his quick intellect got everyone away from the district.

Yoshida proceeded to follow behind Kenzo.

Kenzo said as loud as possible "They're all out of the way!"

Everyone stood in silence

Danzai smiled with an intent to kill.

Danzai's power continued to leak through his sword as he charged through with his latent blood power barely making it out alive as he suffered from some offence with small assistance from Kenzo and Yoshida standing on top of the soldiers. The whole district fell apart at the hands of the three's destruction.

Everyone that was evacuated outside came back in to see the aftermath of the fight.

"Listen all of you, I have one thing to say, the Sasaki bloodline will fall by our hands only and you'll all be set free," said the courageous trio.

Kenzo saw Lana again saying before he goes to the other side is that "I'll be back for you" he said.

"I'll be waiting," Lana said joyfully

The three men get to the other side on proceeding with their journey. Little did they know one soldier remained alive making a report.

What will happen next?

Chapter 4: Second Stage Training

One week had passed since Kenzo, Danzai and Yoshida got past the other side of the Sasaki District, doing what they do best right now... walking.

"I want to see Lana, "Kenzo said

"You'll get to her master after you complete your legacy," Yoshida said.

As the three walked, Danzai was quiet not engaging in conversations. When he decides to speak, he asked Kenzo:

"Kenzo, you must train, I think receiving training from me will benefit you even more," said Danzai bluntly.

"What," said Yoshida and Kenzo

Danzai carefully explained the reason why he suddenly wanted to train, he had second thoughts about the destruction of the Sasaki as

Danzai thought that Kenzo hadn't received enough training and only knows the basic skill, not the advanced aspects of the sword.

Kenzo accepted the training, but he wouldn't have thought the moment he starts, he would feel enormous agony.

"They just started, and this is already the effect of Danzai's training," Yoshida said feeling this will be a while.

What felt like hours to Kenzo was only minutes to Danzai. Every time Kenzo thought he was going to collapse, he thought about the villagers in Nuville giving him strength.

The scenery of Kenzo facing Danzai, as they are about to have a practice scramble. Danzai asked Kenzo one time if he was "Ready"

Kenzo thinks about the time Yoshida trained him. Kenzo nodded and gripped his wooden sword tightening it. "I am Danzai- sensei"

A minute of silence filled up in the air as the two bloodline members are about to commence their battle. A leaf falls, Danzai's wooden sword comes to life and he becomes flawless with his steps. Kenzo's eyes inflated as he witnessed Danzai's speed flourished as if he was a founder of the blade.

A gale of strikes struck upon Kenzo, who just barely got away from suffering each of Danzai's offences.

Danzai's sword brewed through the air, sending instantaneous and terrifying strike blows. Kenzo's heart pounded as he struggles to keep up with Danzai's level of skill.

He moved as he tried to counter Danzai but as he goes on he becomes more strained.

Sweat rained on Kenzo fighting against the strong one Danzai. While they were fighting, Yoshida watched as he sees a difference in Kenzo comparing him now to when he trained him. However, history was repeating of Kenzo being outclassed.

The moment Danzai let his guard down, Kenzo wrapped his leg around Danzai as he lost his balance.

"Gotcha," Kenzo said

Kenzo was ready to strike down Danzai. An occurrence happened and Kenzo felt something was behind him.

"Are you sure about that?" Danzai said

Kenzo looked behind him to Danzai's blade pointed at the back of his neck, this became a mistake as the role reversed. Danzai swiftly lifted himself, gripping Kenzo's kimono and slamming him down on the ground in a fast motion.

The final touch was Danzai's sword pointed at Kenzo's skull.

"You spoke at the wrong time," said Danzai

"I did?" Kenzo in confusion

Yoshida continued watching them "For a moment, I thought Kenzo had him just now. Maybe it is too early for that as Danzai is still too experienced, it won't just take a mere day for an inexperienced fighter to do anything against an experienced one. Will he progress at a quick pace, or will it be a slow one?" Yoshida said to himself

Danzai looks into Kenzo's eyes, wondering "Can he defeat Lei Sasaki?"

No matter what, Danzai tried to assure himself he can do it as it is factual for an Ogushi to have the best percentage of defeating a strong Sasaki bloodline member.

"Keep it together Danzai, you know full on well you don't have the facilities of defeating him. Only Kenzo does he is the only one that can do it even if you have to swallow your pride and accept the fact your blood couldn't get the job done" he said in his mind.

He went back to his regular stance telling "Kenzo get up, we're going again."

"What!" Kenzo said

"You heard me no what's, buts or anything. I want absolute silence from you all we do is train. Do you understand me?" said a motivated Danzai

Kenzo didn't understand the change of tone in Danzai. The urge of a raging burning spirit from Danzai touched Kenzo slowly making its way out.

"I understand, Danzai-sensei," he said

The two quickly resumed their training as of now, the results did not differ for him.

"Well, the determination remains in Kenzo. Why wouldn't, Ogushi's blood runs In him, his father's blood lives on. Lei could never stop that. You may have killed him Lei, but you will face death very soon just you wait." Yoshida said in rage in his head.

✳✳✳

Before they knew it a day had passed by them. The training continues. Kenzo's attitude towards fighting had begun to evolve, he was becoming a hungered beast that craved a meal out of its prey.

Kenzo's hunger was a battle, Danzai saw through this mirroring him to Lei and Alina, this made him think of Kenzo's upcoming battle and whether it affects him tremendously driving the world back to peace or will it lead to more destruction at Kenzo's hands.

The belief of it was uneasy for Danzai. He felt shameful thinking of it but he didn't let that possibility stay in his head for too long and focused back on what was important.

It was barbaric for the inexperienced one who's never felt such agony in his body.

"I do not know how long I can take this," Kenzo said grieving in pain

"You better not be quitting on me, clear all the thoughts in your head think of nothing else?" Danzai said

No matter, Kenzo ran out of energy and collapsed.

Waking up hours later in the rain he was covered by shelter.

The moment he woke up he was asked "if he was okay" but he didn't answer them

He said:

"Look guys I need a breather if you mind" as he walks to get his own space.

Danzai was about to say something but Yoshida said "Let him be"

Kenzo walked off along a dirt path that led him to see a sign saying "Shama" which represented an unfinished construction of a village with joyful people despite their lifestyle living in the current era.

The narrow broken-down streets with rock houses. Black and red bananas waved in the wind. Taking himself to absorb the atmosphere around him. Kenzo found a quiet spot under the shade of a tree.

He allowed his mind to travel, closing his eyes and reflecting on his current journey. Kenzo understood the importance of taking time for himself, he needed to meditate to rejuvenate his spirit. The Ogushi one opened back his eyes making a silent vow to himself that he will be back for his village.

"You will complete this," he said

From a distance, Yoshida and Danzai stood tall on top of trees watching him despite Kenzo saying he wanted some space for himself. "Yoshida, tell me what you think of

Kenzo," Danzai asked. A minute of silence lingered between them.

"Kenzo's spirit and blood shine brightly but if he goes off track, he will dramatically end up being in a dangerous pathway. That's what you've been thinking haven't you" Yoshida asked Danzai

"I would be lying if I wasn't thinking that"

They continue to watch him.

"He carries the weight of defeating Lei Sasaki, something that he desires to do. However, I fear that the pressure on him might be too great for him to handle in the future" Danzai explained to Yoshida

Yoshida nodded "will just have to wait for what comes, but I am certain he will remain the same." He said as the two let Kenzo be.

✳✳✳

Kenzo comes back coming with a new attitude ready to face Danzai in their second practice bout in the blistering rain.

"He's different," Yoshida said

Kenzo grabbed his wooden sword and told Danzai "I want round two now" as the rain continues to fall on them.

Danzai stares at him with excitement.

"Your attitude changes again Ogushi one. We begin the rematch now!" Danzai said

With a swift motion, Kenzo lunged forward, his strikes a flurry of precision and speed. His movements were fluid, each swing of his blade propelled by newfound confidence. Danzai, though taken aback by the intensity of Kenzo's attacks, met each strike with his characteristic grace and skill.

The clash of their swords reverberated throughout the training grounds, echoing the fierce determination within Kenzo's heart. He no longer moved purely on instinct but with a calculated strategy, exploiting openings and anticipating Danzai's counters. Kenzo's progress was evident in every strike, every parry, and every graceful counter

He recognized the fire burning within Kenzo, the passion that had propelled him forward. The seasoned warrior could see the reflection of his teachings in Kenzo's technique, woven together with the young warrior's unique style.

Unexpectedly Danzai used:

MUSENGE LIGHTING STRIKE!

A huge flash went with Kenzo tanking the Musenge bloodline power from the Danzai. He couldn't believe his eyes and so could Yoshida but…

"Well done." Danzai and Yoshida said

Everyone froze.

Kenzo raised his fist in the air

Breathing heavily, Kenzo stood tall, his chest heaving with exertion. He looked at Danzai, his eyes gleaming with gratitude and respect. "Thank you, Danzai-sensei. Your guidance and faith in me have shaped me into the warrior I am today. I still have much to learn, but I am determined to continue growing."

Danzai was now assured that Kenzo will not go down the dark path.

So, is this training done now? We still must go to the Ogushi land.

Both having a positive attitude they set out to the Ogushi land, where Kenzo will finally learn everything.

Chapter 5: Uncovering Everything

Four days later after Danzai had trained him, The three embarked on their journey to the fallen Ogushi Land Kenzo's birthplace. The path they took was a horrible one as they had to go through more forests, rivers and horrific mountains. Yoshida was doing this for Kenzo's sake as he will be able to grasp who he is and how this can unlock the power within.

Despite the hardships they were going through a resilient Yoshida continued to lead the way to the Ogushi Land. "Come on you two we can't stop now" he said.

The terrains became craggy as they approached the outskirts of the fallen Ogushi land. The air was heavy with a sense of foreboding, yet their resolve seized to fade away.

The journey was demanding both mental and physical willpower which they still had to them.

"I want to know who I am." Said Kenzo in his mind

As they neared their destination, the fallen Ogushi Land. The once pleasant place is now covered in battle scars taken two decades ago, bruises etched into the Earth.

They had got to their destination witnessing the Ogushi Land being in a state of complete sadness.

"So, this is my birthplace Yoshida?" Kenzo said

"It's a shame I didn't get to witness the greatness of this land," Danzai said taking in the disastrous air that fills the place

The sight was heart-wrenching for Yoshida.

"It pains me to see this place again."

Crumbled structures and broken walls stood as a silent witness to a glorious past now lost to time.

Kenzo's eyes swept across the desolate landscape suddenly getting visions of when it prospered.

Kenzo didn't understand his emotions once he and the others arrived there.

"What am I seeing," he said to himself

Kenzo sat down on the crumbled floor looking up witnessing a lonely place in desperate need of a friend.

Yoshida as he calls Danzai and Kenzo and raises his hands telling them "Danzai and Kenzo what you see before your eyes is the Ogushi Land in its relentless state done by the Sasaki.

Yoshida pointed at Kenzo "This is where you'll learn everything as I said a million times, but it won't be told by me it will be told by your ancestors."

"What do you mean ancestors?" said the confused Kenzo

Yes, what do you mean by ancestors? How does that work, Kenzo speaking to his ancestors" said Danzai

"Come on Danzai, You should have a little idea of what I can be talking about" Yoshida tried to make him think

Danzai as he was about to speak froze just understood what Yoshida was trying to say.

"I see now it all makes sense why you wanted him to come here so badly for Kenzo."

"You understand what he is saying?"

Danzai takes a seat and allows Yoshida to explain what he wants to say.

Yoshida leaned forward; his eyes filled with conviction. "It starts with quieting your mind, just as we did during our journey here. Through meditation and deep introspection, you create a space within yourself where you can connect with the spiritual realm. Your ancestors will communicate with you through whispers, visions, and intuition. Trust your instincts, Kenzo, and let their guidance flow through you."

Danzai, who had been quietly observing the conversation, spoke up for the first time. "It sounds like a powerful and sacred practice. Are you certain Kenzo is ready for this?"

Yoshida nodded, his gaze steady and unwavering. "Kenzo has shown immense strength and resilience throughout our journey. He has a burning desire to understand his true self. I believe he is ready to embark on this spiritual journey and embrace the wisdom of his ancestors."

Kenzo took a deep breath, his doubts gradually transforming into a sense of anticipation. "I am willing to try, Yoshida. If there's a chance to uncover my true identity and find my purpose, I want to seize it."

Yoshida smiled warmly, a spark of pride in his eyes. "That is the spirit, Kenzo. Embrace the legacy of your ancestors, and let their voices guide you. The fallen Ogushi Land will bear witness to the rebirth of your true self."

Kenzo closed his eyes

"Will this work?" Danzai asked

Kenzo reopened his eyes seeing nothing but darkness no Yoshida and Danzai in his sight what he sees is a bright light shaped like a door. He slowly heads towards the light and once he got near it everything suddenly became even brighter once the brightness cooled down he looked at a scene which will never leave his head.

It was the scene of him finally confirming he was a part of the Ogushi bloodline as he saw lookalikes of him of different ages and gender living happily in their spiritual world after death.

"This is real, Yoshida and Danzai were right about this I am a part of the Ogushi Clan!" he said excitedly

He ran around hugging the random Ogushi ancestors making them very confused saying "Who is this guy?"

He couldn't stop running to explore but then quickly remembered what he was here for.

"Right, I can't get too carried away, there's still I must do"- he said

"Do you think he is there?" asked Danzai

"The fact that he hasn't opened his eyes yet says it all don't you think." Said Yoshida

"I guess you're right"

✳✳✳

Standing In the centre, Kenzo shouts saying:

"EVERYONE HERE, LISTEN TO ME!"

They all look at Kenzo

"I AM HERE TO ANNOUNCE THAT, I AM THE ONLY BLOODLINE MEMBER OF OUR CLAN THE OGUSHI. MY NAME IS KENZO OGUSHI!" He said courageously

The whole bloodline stared at him but two people were coming out of cotton. The two people were a man and a female looking remarkably similar to Kenzo.

Tears welled up in Kenzo's eyes as he realized it at first glance. "Are... Are you my parents?" he choked out, his voice trembling with emotion.

The woman, with tears of joy in her eyes, stepped forward and nodded. "Yes, Kenzo.

We are your parents. We have watched over you from this realm, watching you grow."

The man, Kenzo's father, spoke with a mixture of pride and sorrow in his voice. "We regret that we could not be with you physically, but we have always been here in spirit, cheering you on, my son."

Overwhelmed with emotion, Kenzo ran towards them and embraced them tightly. "I never knew you existed, but I always felt like something was missing in my life," he said, his voice trembling. "Now I understand. I've always been connected to the Ogushi bloodline, to you."

His mother caressed his cheek gently. "You are a part of us, Kenzo. The strength, courage, and determination you possess are traits passed down through generations of our family. We are proud of the person you have become."

His father added, "You are our legacy, Kenzo. Carry the Ogushi name with honour, and let our spirit guide you on your path."

***

Yoshida and Danzai witness tears come out of Kenzo's eyes

"He's met them now hasn't he," Danzai asked

"Yes, Danzai… he has" he said trying to hold his tears.

***

Under the resplendent moonlight, Kenzo sat cross-legged in a secluded chamber within the fallen Ogushi Land. His father, the former leader of the Ogushi Clan, stood before him, his eyes reflecting the weight of centuries of history.

"Kenzo," his father began, his voice carrying a mixture of pride and sorrow. "Our bloodline, the Ogushi Clan, has always been shrouded in secrecy. We possess a unique gift, the ability to channel the spirits of our ancestors, granting us enhanced strength in battle. But we are not the only bloodlines in this world."

He took a deep breath, and the room seemed to hum with anticipation. "The Musenge, known for their lightning attacks, and the Sasaki, who use their blood to enhance their samurai strengths, have been both allies and adversaries throughout history."

Kenzo's eyes widened, intrigued by the revelation. "How are we connected to them?"

His father sighed; his gaze distant yet pained. "Many generations ago, a bond was forged between the Ogushi and the Musenge. Together, we fought side by side against common threats, and our families became intertwined through friendships and marriages."

"However," he continued, his expression darkening, "ambition and envy led to discord, and the Sasaki Emperor, Lei, sought to control both our bloodlines. He craved power and believed that by uniting the Musenge and the Sasaki, he could control the Ogushi as well."

Kenzo's heart sank at the thought of the malevolent Sasaki Emperor. "What happened then, Father?"

With a heavy breath, his father revealed the painful truth. "Lei Sasaki, with his right hand, Alina Sasaki, betrayed us. They orchestrated a treacherous attack that targeted the heart of our clan. Many brave Ogushi warriors were lost that day, and I fell in battle, unable to protect our family."

"But Yoshida was there to take me safety," Kenzo said

"Yes that's true," his mother and father said

Kenzo's body starts to feel funny becoming aware his time in this realm will end he asked his father one thing.

"Father and Mother, Yoshida told me about a sword that I'll find in our land, do you know about it."

His father said, "Of course, I do remember I was the one that told Yoshida about it being deep underground you have to use your gut feeling to find it."

Kenzo's body starts to disappear.

"Well, son it seems your time here is over." His father said

"Remember, my son no matter what we will always be proud of you." His tearful mother said.

Every Ogushi wished him "Goodluck!" waving at him

Kenzo woke up from the other world instantly using his strength to break down the ground seeing a glowing item he pulls it out to be a crimson, blue katana that was built for Kenzo in the future.

There was no need for Kenzo's wooden sword anymore he now required what he needs for the Sasaki. The wind blew around him to showcase the tremendous power that was slowly breaking his limits.

"Kenzo, Is it time now," Danzai and Yoshida said with anticipation

"IT IS TIME NOW MY FRIENDS, NOW WE GO TO THE EMPEROR AND KILL THIS BASTARD ONCE AND FOR ALL!"

Within the grand halls of the Sasaki Emperor's palace, a chilling aura of power and authority permeated the air. Lei Sasaki, the ruthless and ambitious ruler, sat upon his ornate throne, his eyes narrowed with cunning.

One of his loyal soldiers knelt before him, his body bearing the scars of a fierce battle. "Your Majesty," the soldier began, his voice trembling with both fear and reverence, "I have grave news to report. During the recent conflict with the Ogushi Clan twenty-one years, one of their bloodline members survived. He escaped the Sasaki district and is still alive."

Lei Sasaki's eyes flashed with a mixture of anger and surprise. "A survivor from the Ogushi Clan? That is unacceptable. They were supposed to be eradicated," he growled, clenching his fist.

Could this be Mahi's child by any chance?

Lei said in desperation to his soldier.

Without hesitation, Lei called upon his right hand, Alina Sasaki, a formidable warrior known for her cunning and ruthlessness. "Alina," he said, his voice low and dangerous, "you are to find this survivor and bring him to me, alive if possible, but dead if necessary. I want no loose ends threatening the Sasaki dynasty."

Alina nodded, her steely gaze never wavering. "Consider it done, Your Majesty," she replied with unwavering confidence. "I will hunt down this Ogushi bloodline member and bring him to you."

As she departed, Lei watched her with a sense of satisfaction. Alina was his most trusted ally and an expert tracker. He knew that she would stop at nothing to complete her mission.

Now that Kenzo has required his blade how will things turn out for him and his group?

Chapter 6: A Sad Loss

The Journey of now knowing everything from his Mother and Father, Kenzo now fully makes a must to kill Lei Sasaki as he, Danzai and Yoshida are heading to the closing stage of their journey. Between all three men, it was a mix of excitement and fear.

It took them three hours until Yoshida realised "This is it we're nearly there to kill that bastard!" he said energetically

"Yeah" also commented

"I will complete this for my bloodline!" Kenzo said in his head

As they were closing in, shadows seemed to spread at a tremendous rate.

"Wait guys something feels very odd, draw your weapons" Yoshida whispered to his allies warning them.

Kenzo and Danzai gripped their prestigious blades to strike anything worth an enemy. "I can feel the power," Kenzo said

The group continued their movements while watching their surroundings, so they won't be the ones being struck down "Remember people stay focused" Kenzo said

Just as they thought they had eluded detection, they found themselves surrounded by a group of Sasaki soldiers, led by a formidable woman with piercing eyes and an aura of authority. It was Alina Sasaki, Lei's right hand.

The heroic trio was stunned and frightened as she appeared out of nowhere. "WHAT THE HECK!" said Danzai

"IT'S HER INNIT," Danzai said

Alina didn't take her eyes off them. "Let's look what we have here I'm assuming you're the Ogushi, Yoshida the messenger and a Musenge here all right in front of me"

"Is this the right hand you've been talking about Yoshida?" Kenzo asked

"Yes it is that moron"

"That's not nice Yoshida, perhaps I should cut off that little face of yours. I will just get to the point you and the Musenge user don't matter to me I just need the Ogushi one" she said

"AND HOW DO YOU KNOW AN OGUSHI IS ALIVE!" Said Danzai and Yoshida

"Simple one of our soldiers reported back to Lei and explained the situation of what happened In the district because you three failed to kill all of the men there. That's all." She explained

Danzai immediately felt guilty as he thought he took care of everyone in the district.

"Well, what are we waiting for, guess I have no options but to fight. My men stay down and hold your position I will take off this." She said with confidence

In her fighting position, she stared them down.

Kenzo, Yoshida, and Danzai - stood ready for their confrontation with Alina. As the battle commenced, Yoshida unholstered his bow and notched an arrow, his eyes locked onto their formidable adversary.

With the twang of the bowstring, the arrow whizzed through the air, seeking its target. Alina moved with uncanny grace, deflecting the arrow effortlessly with her blade. She advanced on them with speed and precision, her movements like a deadly dance.

Kenzo's eyes narrowed, and he lunged forward, wielding the Ogushi blade with a newfound determination. His strikes were fierce, but Alina deftly parried each one, her skill proving her worth as Lei's right-hand warrior.

Danzai, ever the agile and adaptable fighter, moved in and out of the fray, attempting to find an opening in Alina's defences. But she seemed to anticipate his every move, countering with a fluidity that left him momentarily disoriented.

"We can't let her overpower us," Yoshida called out, his voice steady even amid battle. "Work together, find your openings."

The three regrouped, their eyes locked onto Alina. They moved in unison, attacking from different angles, testing her defences. Despite their efforts, Alina's skillset remained unmatched, her movements a symphony of lethal strikes.

Kenzo gritted his teeth, channelling the power of the Ogushi bloodline. His strikes grew stronger, fuelled by his determination to protect his allies and honour Yoshida's sacrifice.

Yoshida continued to fire arrows with incredible precision, but Alina seemed to predict each shot, effortlessly avoiding them. His brows furrowed in concentration as he adjusted his aim, refusing to give up.

Danzai, always the strategist, sought to exploit Alina's patterns, but she was an elusive target, slipping out of reach with ease. He fought with unwavering determination, not willing to back down.

As the battle intensified, Kenzo's mind flashed back to his training with Yoshida and Danzai, to the countless hours of practice, and the lessons learned. He realized that the true strength of their bond lay in their ability to trust each other and fight as a team.

Yoshida, Danzai, trust me," Kenzo called out, a glint of determination in his eyes.

With a shared understanding, the trio synchronized their movements, attacking in a coordinated assault. Yoshida's arrows pinned Alina in place, Danzai created distractions, and Kenzo seized the opportunity to strike.

Their combined effort pushed Alina back, momentarily breaking through her defences. The Sasaki warrior's eyes flashed with surprise; her superiority finally being challenged.

In that brief opening, Kenzo's blade connected with Alina's, causing a resounding clang. The force of the impact sent Alina stumbling back, and the trio took a moment to catch their breath.

"You fight well," Alina conceded, her breaths heavy. "But this isn't over."

She called out:

SASAKI TECHNIQUE; THOUSAND PIERCING BLADES!

Her techniques pierced through their skin making their pupils in their eyes becoming completely blank. All three men fell to the ground leaking out their blood in battle.

"Struggling to speak Danzai said "This is a pain"

"She's too strong, even with my newfound strength it's not enough," Kenzo said

"You see, all three can't go against me," she said in the distance chuckling

As Kenzo, Yoshida, and Danzai lay on the ground, their bodies battered and bloodied, Alina approached them with an air of triumph. She towered over them, a cruel smile on her lips.

"You fought valiantly, I'll give you that," Alina taunted, her voice dripping with arrogance. "But the difference in power between us is too great. Lei's vision will prevail, and there's nothing you can do to stop it."

"I don't recall caring I won't stop," he said

Yoshida was shivering from holding his bow and arrow hanging on to his last breath.

Alina scoffed "You think that brat can stop the Sasaki's existence"

Danzai struggled to sit up, a grimace of pain crossing his face. "You may have the power now, but we'll find a way to stop you and bring justice to those you've oppressed.

"Oh, shut up!"

Alina's blade slashed Yoshida making him fall to his knees.

"YOSHIDA!" Kenzo and Danzai cried out

Nearly fading away he tells them "Guys it's the end of the road for me, Danzai take care of Kenzo for me as I have now failed his father and Kenzo remember, fulfil your legacy." Yoshida said giving them a thumbs up

Alina finishes Yoshida Give him another blow.

Yoshida was now lifeless and no longer in the world of the living.

At first experience, Kenzo felt so much pain he passed out not getting any chance to mourn Yoshida who had guided him through his journey so far.

✳✳✳

As Kenzo's eyes fluttered open with the remaining tears left in his eyes, he found himself in a dimly lit chamber, his surroundings unfamiliar. As his vision cleared, he realized that he was lying on a cold stone floor, bound by heavy chains that restricted his movements with Danzai beside him.

"DAMN, DAMN DAMMIT!, YOSHIDA DIDN'T DESERVE THAT!" Kenzo said

A figure stepped out from the shadows, revealing the imposing presence of Lei Sasaki, the Sasaki Emperor. His cold, calculating eyes locked onto Kenzo's, and a sinister smile curved on his lips.

"So, you're the thing that's been bothering me for nearly two decades, Nice to meet you I am

Lei Sasaki" he said staring into Kenzo's heart and eyes.

Chapter 7: The Confrontation

In the chamber, there was a crackle of Intensity between Lei and Kenzo. Kenzo's eyes lightened with rage he had never felt before,

Not giving any time to mourn Yoshida, he already set his sight to avenge his death. Lei's eyes stayed calculated with Kenzo as he gives him a hideous smile.

"I hope you know I'm going to kill you," Kenzo said viciously

"Is that so, well then try to break out of those shackles and do that. Oh, right you can't" Lei said

He gets closer

"Even if you did manage to break yourself from those shackles the chances of me beating to a pulp is ninety percent". Kenzo responded saying "So what about the one per cent, that ninety-nine per cent can just reduce to zero."

"Is that so?" Danzai said

Danzai, lying bruised and battered on the floor, tried to rise. "Kenzo, don't let his words get to you. He's trying to provoke you."

Kenzo looked around curious as to why seeing his sword next to him and Danzai's on his side. "Why did you let us keep our swords? Is that how much you think you can beat me and Danzai?"

"Of course, I am the strongest after all."

Being delayed in his reactions Lei approached Kenzo and delivered a mocking kick to his ribs, causing him to wince in pain. "What's the matter? Can't handle a little pain?"

"Kenzo!" Danzai shouted, his shackles preventing him from helping his friend.

"Don't worry Danzai you'll get yours soon," Lei said

Kenzo staggered back on his feet causing annoyance and amusement to Lei. "You bastard you still want to go?" Kenzo replied saying "The way how I see things right now there's no rush in this eventually today will be your last day of taking a breath. I guarantee that to you Sasaki Emperor Lei"

Lei struck again at Kenzo.

"Stop this madness!" Danzai said

"There's no way out for you. Your fate is sealed, just like the rest of your pitiful clan."

Danzai's eyes blazed with defiance. "You won't break us. The Ogushi bloodline will endure, and you will pay for your crimes."

Infuriated by Danzai's words, Lei turned his attention to him, delivering a series of brutal blows. Danzai's body convulsed with pain, but he refused to yield.

As Kenzo struggled to his feet once more, his vision blurred with tears of frustration and anger. He felt the weight of his shackles, the chains that held him back from defending his friend and avenging Yoshida's death.

Once again Lei struck Kenzo down

Alina enters the chamber

Kenzo and Danzai don't take their eyes off her. Alina smirked at them as they look like two loose cannons

"My bad how rude of me, what are your names you two?"

"Our names, now you ask of us our names! Well, my name is Danzai you already know the second name" said Danzai

"My name is Kenzo!, you're welcome"

"Interesting names. Now that I know your names do you Kenzo and Danzai want to know a story about me?"

They both said, "Not really, we only have time to kill you."

Lei and Alina laugh

"Well, I'm going to tell anyway, before me my father was once the leader of the Sasaki bloodline, a man revered for his strength and skill in battle. But he grew obsessed with power, always seeking ways to become even stronger, funny it sounds just like me."

"So, you took advantage of your own father's thirst for power? When you were already strong as you were" Kenzo said

"Oh, Kenzo and Danzai, It was quite easy for me and Alina just had to kill him and take his blood to amplify ourselves even more not just him but secretly taking in the blood of others in the Sasaki Bloodline. Besides my father was a prick so there was no hesitation in doing it."

"You're sick you know that right," said Danzai

"I know I am. AND I LOVE IT" Lei said

"But now I have no use talking to you migrants anymore, Alina dispose of these fools"

"As you wish"

As Alina is about to finish them off.

a sudden commotion outside the chamber caught everyone's attention. The sound of clashing weapons and battle cries echoed through the halls,

"What's going on out there!"

"By the sounds of those battle cry, it appears the Musenge bloodline are here." Said Yoshida

Deal with them," Lei commanded Alina, his voice seething with rage and frustration.

Alina nodded, a ruthless determination taking over her features. She turned back to Kenzo and Danzai, her eyes gleaming with malice. "It seems like we'll have to continue our little game later," she taunted, her hand gripping her blade tightly.

As Alina left the chamber Lei went to his throne grabbing his crimson red blade from the seat and elegantly shifting his sword arm to arm preparing to end his opposition for good.

Wasting no time Lei with his quick speed aimed for Kenzo's neck, however, it backfired as   Kenzo aimed his shackles towards Lei's blade cutting them off completely.

Kenzo quickly grabbed his sword at the exact moment cutting off Danzai's as well to add on he attempted to strike him, but Lei blocked Kenzo's offence pushing him far back.

There was a moment of silence as Lei was surprised

Both noble warriors come out of their chamber

"The Final Stage starts now!"

As the story is coming to a close how will the story end?

Chapter 8: The Final Stage

In the heart of the Sasaki Empire, the remaining Musenge Bloodline members stood firm, facing a sea of Sasaki soldiers. The air crackled with tension as both sides prepared for the inevitable clash.

"You morons will pay for the years of suffering you have caused to our people; your names shall be part of my blade!" said the Musenge bloodline

"That's not going to happen will just send you nicely to the upper room where you can see your dead families!" said

As the Sasaki soldiers charged, the Musenge Bloodline members fought back with skill and unity. Their bloodline passed down through generations, granted them a deep connection to the element. They wielded their powers like an unstoppable force of nature, each warrior complementing the others' abilities.

The Sasaki soldiers, though numerous, were taken aback by the ferocity of the Musenge Bloodline's resistance.

MUSENGE LIGHTNING STRIKE!

MUSENGE 2000 CONSECUTIVE STRIKES!

SASAKI WHIRLIND TORNANO!

SASAKI ONE INCH IMPALER!

Techniques were being released everywhere in the chaotic battle

With each swing of their swords, the Musenge Bloodline members stood firm, protecting each other as if they were family, which, in truth, they were. Their bond was their strength, and it fuelled their determination to stand against the tyranny of the Sasaki Empire.

As the battle raged on, Alina made her way to the battlefield, her eyes fixed on the Musenge warriors. Her calculated demeanour remained unchanged as she observed their display of lightning prowess.

Alina made a quick assessment of the situation, recognizing the threat posed by the Musenge Bloodline's lightning abilities. She knew she had to approach the battle strategically, seeking the best opportunity to strike and dismantle their unity.

The battlefield crackled with energy as both sides continued to clash. The remaining Musenge Bloodline warriors were a formidable force to be reckoned with, using their lightning powers to devastating effect.

***

Back at Lei's palace, Kenzo looked at Danzai with a determined gaze saying "Danzai"

"Yeah" He responded

"Go fight with your people," Kenzo said firmly,

"What," said Danzai

"You're needed out there, and I know you'll lead them well. I will handle Lei."

Danzai hesitated for a moment, torn between his loyalty to Kenzo and his responsibility to the Musenge Bloodline. But he understood that Kenzo had a personal score to settle with Lei, and he trusted his friend's capabilities despite their battered state.

"All right, Kenzo perform justice for us," Danzai said

Danzai leaves them be and makes his way to his family

The only two men in the palace were Kenzo and Lei.

Lei gets himself ready despite all the trash talking he knows this fight that's been destined might take a while

"Ready when you're… Ogushi Survivor Kenzo!"

Both men run towards each with their charging up their respective bloodline energy. As blades clashed the area trembled eventually causing a bright explosion

The remaining Musenge Bloodline members fought valiantly, holding their ground with tough determination.

Alina saw an opportunity to strike, and she lunged forward with deadly intent.

"YOU ARE FINISHED!" Alina said with a psychotic face

However, just as she was about to deliver a decisive blow, a sudden gust of wind and crackling lightning diverted her attention.

Danzai appeared out of nowhere blocking her strike from doing any more damage to his blood.

"WHAT, YOU GOT OUT. HOW IS THIS POSSIBLE" Alina said in shock

"OF COURSE, I GOT OUT OTHERWISE… WHY AM I STANDING HERE BLOCKING YOUR SWORD YOU BAFOON," Danzai answered

"Thank you master Danzai." The Musenge soldiers said

"No, I must thank you guys for coming out here for me without this surprise visit who knows me and Kenzo's head would have been chopped off. As again thank you my blood"

The Musenge try to contain their emotions

Danzai focuses his attention back on Alina

"Touching Conversation, but the way how I see we're in a middle of a war so patch it up."

Without a word, Danzai charged forward, releasing a powerful surge of lightning from his blade. Alina swiftly evaded his attack, but Danzai continued his assault, refusing to give her a moment's rest.

Their blades clashed with intense force, the sound of steel meeting steel echoing through the battlefield. The Musenge soldiers watched in awe as their leader fought with incredible skill and strength.

Alina's attacks were swift and precise, and she seemed to anticipate Danzai's every move. However, Danzai's lightning abilities gave him an advantage in speed and agility, allowing him to match her blows and retaliate with equal ferocity.

The battle between the two bloodline warriors intensified, their power crackling in the air. Danzai's determination and love for his people fuelled his lightning strikes, while Alina's sadistic nature drove her to push her bloodline abilities to the limit.

As the fight continued, Danzai's lightning strikes became more potent, and he managed to land a powerful blow on Alina, sending her stumbling back. But Alina refused to back down, her eyes glinting with malice.

"You're stronger than I expected, Musenge," Alina said, wiping the blood from her cheek. "But you won't defeat me that easily."

Danzai's chest heaved with exertion, but he remained steadfast. He knew that he had to keep fighting, not only for his people but also to protect the legacy of the Musenge Bloodline.

Alina's eyes widened with surprise and fear, realizing that she had underestimated Danzai's true strength. She attempted to evade the attack, but the lightning seemed to follow her every move.

In a final, desperate effort, Alina gathered her bloodline power and struck back at Danzai with all her might. The clash of their abilities created a blinding flash of light, engulfing the battlefield.

The flashing lights faded away with both Soldiers being heavily damaged as bruises and cuts were added to them.

But Alina still had strength in her

Alina's sadistic grin remained on her face, despite the pain she felt. "Is that all you've got, Danzai? I expected more from the esteemed leader of the Musenge Bloodline," she taunted.

Civilians were watching the chaos lost on what was happening as everything. The actions were too fast to comprehend

"Don't worry I am far from done. I won't rest until I see you and the other on the ground lifeless but right now you're my priority while Kenzo handles the big man."

As the battle raged on, Danzai's lightning strikes intensified, and he managed to land a series of powerful blows on Alina. Each strike seemed to drain her strength, but she refused to back down, her eyes burning with a fierce determination.

Despite her wounds, Alina launched a desperate counterattack, unleashing a devastating bloodline technique that sent shockwaves through the battlefield. Danzai struggled to defend against the onslaught, his body pushed to its limits.

"I have one more arsenal in the tank that I can use to put you down for good"

"So do I"

The battle is coming to a close. What are the final moves that both oppositions hold?

Chapter 9: The Final Stage Finale

The Ground Beneath them shook as the two mighty sword masters showcased the aura of their blood. Danzai's lightning surged, sparks and crackles enveloping him like a living storm. His determination to protect his people and end the suffering they endured fuelled his attack. He knew that this moment could change the fate of the Musenge Bloodline forever.

While Alina displayed a wavy malicious aura symbolising her character.

The battlefield fell silent for a split second as both warriors reached their maximum potential

"THIS ENDS NOW!"

Then, with a primal scream, they released their respective attacks, creating a cataclysmic clash of bloodline energies.

The ground shook violently, and shockwaves rippled through the air, sending dust and debris soaring into the sky. The force of the collision was so intense that it shook the very foundation of the Sasaki Empire.

As the dust and debris settled, it revealed the outcome of what had happened.

Alina showed an expression of defeat speaking in fear "This is not right; this can't be the end of me!" she staggered back falling on her back as her body had now lost its soul.

Alina was no more

As Alina stood tall Danzai stood tall despite his severe injuries, his mind tells him to rest but his body tells him to stand.

"I did It, now everything falls to Kenzo. Yoshida, we defeated Alina just for you" He said dropping one tear

Danzai's strength gave way, and he collapsed to the ground, unconscious. The Musenge soldiers rushed to his side, their cheers mixed with concern for their leader's well-being.

"DANZAI, YOU DID IT!" His fellow blood said

Meanwhile, in a different part of the battlefield, the legendary battle between Kenzo and Lei was already in motion. Sparks

of bloodline power crackled around them, as the two mighty sword masters faced off against each other.

The ground trembled beneath their feet as they charged at each other, their swords clashing with a force that echoed across the battlefield. Their movements were a dance of deadly precision, each strike calculated to test the other's strength and skill.

Lei's blade gleamed with blood, a testament to his mastery of the Sasaki Bloodline's power to manipulate his life force into a weapon. His attacks were swift and precise, aiming to strike at Kenzo's weaknesses and exploit any opening he could find.

As the legendary battle raged on, the battlefield around them seemed to cause an earthquake in response to their bloodline energies clashing. The remaining Sasaki soldiers could hear the loud sounds of the battle but couldn't witness it.

Outside the epic battlefield, Kenzo had managed to push the battle to the outskirts of the Sasaki Empire's territory. His determination to avenge his fallen clan and protect the Musenge Bloodline gave him the strength to continue fighting despite his fatigue.

As he clashed swords with Lei, their bloodline energies created shockwaves that shook the very earth around them. Trees swayed, and the ground trembled as if echoing the intensity of their battle. The clash of their blades resonated throughout the entire land, a testament to the legendary showdown taking place.

But amidst the chaos and destruction, something caught Kenzo's eye. A group of civilians from nearby villages had gathered, drawn to the scene by the sheer magnitude of the battle. Among them was an elderly woman whose eyes widened in disbelief as she saw Kenzo.

"No, that white hair, it couldn't be an Ogushi people" she whispered

The others nodded in agreement, acknowledging that they might be witnessing the last living descendant of the fabled Ogushi Clan. The weight of this realization filled the air with Reverence.

Lei was now having enough of this fight he did the favour of doing something Kenzo could not prepare himself for.

"This is child's play I'll do the honours of just releasing all three of my strongest techniques on you to end you and your Legacy you small fool"

"What are you talking about!" Kenzo said

"Don't worry you'll see if you're able to see them"

Lei Channelled his energy. The first technique, "Crimson Slash," erupted with a powerful burst of energy as Lei swung his sword with blinding speed. The crimson arc of his blade tore through the air, leaving a trail of destruction in its wake. It was as if a scarlet comet streaked across the battlefield, aiming directly for Kenzo.

Kenzo's eyes widened at the realization of the sheer force behind Lei's attack. Kenzo barely dodged it as it could have caused half his body to be halved. But Lei wasn't done yet. He seamlessly transitioned into his second technique, "Raging Cyclone."

With a fierce twirl of his blood-infused sword, Lei summoned a violent whirlwind of cutting winds. The cyclone roared and spun, threatening to engulf Kenzo in a tempest of blades. The force of the winds was relentless, and Kenzo found himself struggling to maintain his footing which cause a slip-off him suffering from a more ruthless injury.

"COME ON NOW KENZO, I AM NOT DONE!"

A dark aura enveloped Lei as he poured his life force into the blade. The air around them grew heavy as if weighed down by the impending doom of his attack. The ground quaked, and the skies darkened as Lei raised his blood-infused sword.

In one swift motion, he swung the blade, unleashing a shockwave of pure destruction. The "Eclipse of Blood Oblivion" tore through the battlefield like a black wave, obliterating everything in its path. Kenzo had suffered the full force of Lei's strongest technique

The attack was too powerful that Kenzo's eyes went lifeless again with half of his body falling to the ground while the other side of his body shakes its way up to keep standing.

"You see, Kenzo, your pathetic bloodline was never a match for the might of the Sasaki Empire," Lei sneered. "Your mother and father were fools to challenge us, and they paid the ultimate price for their arrogance."

Kenzo's eyes awaken as pure brightest. Lei notices

"Say that again, my people before they died never challenged you all of what is happening in your cause and you only" Kenzo looks up to him slowly raising his head

"SO DON'T YOU DARE TELL ME ABOUT A CHALLENGE, NOW YOU'RE MAKING THIS A PURPOSE FOR MY REASON OF EXISTENCE!"

Kenzo Aura grew pure white with his Ogushi blade as well. Troy was so focused on building his rage that he wasn't being aware of the changes that were happening to him.

His Hair grew length to his back. Lei did not know how to get himself under control as this moment was the day that he built up so much fear.

What he saw was a demon that came to take his soul.

"YOU TOOK EVERYTHING FROM ME, MY PEOPLE AND MY PARENTS WHOM I'LL NEVER GET TO TALK TO AGAIN!" Kenzo said

Lei wasn't paying attention to any of the words Kenzo was saying

"I still have a village to get back, so back to you'll I'll cut to the chase" Kenzo leered

He jumps up high as possible in the air putting both of his hands together and charging one more blow as the decider. Lei saw this and proceeded to laugh it off as he did the same but only he was at the bottom. He jumped charging up his attack from the low ground.

Both gave their final Battle Crys as their blades collided causing a huge distortion between good and evil.

The people watching saw Kenzo as an angel and Lei as a demon who's been fighting for eternity.

As the struggle continues, Lei pushes back but Kenzo is still holding on.

"You see it's no use Kenzo of the Ogushi Clan, you fought well but you still can't beat me. IT'S OVER FOR YOU!"

As all seemed lost for Kenzo. Something caused agony to Lei as he looked behind him it was a bunch of swords pierced behind his back

"YOU DAMN MUSENGE'S!" He said as he coughs out blood

The People began chanting for Kenzo giving him the final piece as Kenzo beat the struggle shattering Lei's blade along with Lei suffering the wraith of the Ogushi blade.

"NO, THIS CAN'T BE, AM THE STRONGEST!"

Lei's body became nothing but ashes concluding this battle

Kenzo gets back down on ground level raising his sword as he returns to his normal self.

"It's finally over," Kenzo said in relief

As the dust settled after the intense battle between Kenzo and Lei, the onlookers could hardly believe what they had witnessed. Lei, the once-feared leader of the Sasaki Empire, had been defeated by the last living descendant of the Ogushi Clan. The people erupted into cheers, chanting Kenzo's name with reverence and gratitude.

The civilians who had gathered to witness the battle rushed to Kenzo's side. They showered him with praise, thanking him for his bravery and for putting an end to Lei's tyranny. Tears of joy streamed down the elderly woman's face as she approached Kenzo.

"You are a true hero," she said, her voice trembling with emotion. "The Ogushi Clan lives on through you"

Others joined in, expressing their gratitude and admiration for Kenzo's strength and determination. The Musenge soldiers also arrived, carrying the injured but conscious Danzai on a stretcher. They cheered for their leader, grateful that he had survived the intense battle with Alina.

As Danzai opened his eyes and saw Kenzo standing tall, his heart swelled with pride. "You did it, Kenzo," he said with a smile. "You saved us all, and your parents' legacy shines brightly through you."

After a few minutes of celebration, Kenzo addressed the remaining Sasaki leaders who were still standing, though shaken by the events that had unfolded. He advised them to drop their weapons and put an end to the bloodshed. Kenzo urged them to choose peace over war and to let go of the past conflicts that had fired so much suffering.

"We don't need more blood spilt on this land," Kenzo said, his voice firm but compassionate. "Let us find a way to coexist and build a future where all bloodlines can thrive without fear."

Slowly, the Sasaki leaders lowered their weapons, realizing the futility of their fight against the united Musenge and Ogushi forces. They saw the strength and unity Kenzo had inspired, and they knew that continuing the war would only bring more destruction to their empire.

Kenzo had done everything he was destined for 21 years now but now he needed to keep his promise.

***

Days Passed from the battles. Kenzo, still recovering from his injuries, made his way back to his village, Nuville. As he approached, the villagers who had taken care of him for the past 21 years welcomed him with open arms and tears of joy.

The sight of their hero returning victorious filled the air with a sense of relief and gratitude. The village was adorned with colourful banners and decorations, and the sound of drums and music filled the air. Kenzo's heart swelled with warmth as he saw the familiar faces of the people who had become his family.

Despite now fulfilling his promise to return. Kenzo did say… he would come back to Lana returning to Lana

"Oh yes, how could I forget" he slapped himself

With determination in his heart, Kenzo set off on a journey to find Lana in the bustling Sasaki District. The path was long and arduous, but the thought of seeing her again kept him going. Along the way, he encountered various challenges and obstacles he faced when he was with Danzai and Yoshida.

Kenzo found himself near the place where he first met Lana. He recalled their conversation and the connection they had shared. It was then that he spotted her, just as mesmerizing as he remembered.

Approaching her cautiously, Kenzo hoped she would remember him. "Lana," he said softly, not wanting to startle her.

Lana turned her eyes widening in surprise as she recognized Kenzo. "You came back," she said, her voice tinged with both disbelief and delight.

"Yes, I couldn't stay away," Kenzo replied, a warm smile spreading across his face. "I couldn't stop thinking about you and the connection we had."

Lana blushed slightly, her usual composed demeanour faltering for a moment. "I must admit, I've been thinking about you too," she admitted, her eyes meeting his with a mix of curiosity and admiration.

While Kenzo was with Lana. Danzai was now taking over the Sasaki Emperor turning him into the complete opposite of Lei's Emperor

"I thought this was your legacy but no you gave it to me. I wonder what you think of this Yoshida" Danzai said cheerfully looking up at the sky

✳✳✳

Kenzo and Lana were holding hands with the villagers at the back of them admiring the night sky spread with stars.

"Hopefully I hope you get the chance to reunite with your family, our family Yoshida. Mother and Father my legacy is now completed" Kenzo said in satisfaction

Kenzo's Legacy was now complete which comes to an ending to this story.

Everyone that suffered years of pain and despair can now rest as the bosses of this evil world… are no more.

THANK YOU FOR READING

As I come to the end of this book, I am filled with immense gratitude for all those who have made this journey possible. To my cherished readers. I am deeply thankful to every one of you who picked up this book and delved into the world of Kenzo, his struggles, and his triumphs. How did you guys feel about the ending and the Overall story?

Nevertheless, I would Like to Thank you for reading once again. There are more to come, my friends and family,

New Projects

Dragon Cry Volume 3

We are thrilled to bring you the long-awaited third instalment of the fantasy series, Dragon Cry! Get ready to immerse yourself in a world of magic, rivalry, and destiny as we delve into the captivating story of Troy Brown and his comrades participating in a tournament where they will go against familiar faces and new faces in his incredible journey in Volume 3.

The Tournament will lead to anticipated battles and destruction as high rewards are given to whomever team wins the whole thing. Do you think Troy and his group have the capabilities to defeat the 40 other participants?

The Veneria Saga: The Power Within

"The Veneria Saga: The Power Within." In this extraordinary tale, ancient warriors' spirits reside within magical artefacts known as Veneria necklaces. Follow the journey of a young orphan named Oliver Reed as he discovers his true destiny after stumbling upon a Veneria necklace, unlocking its incredible power. Embark on an adventure of epic proportions as Oliver embraces his newfound abilities, joining forces with others who share similar gifts. Together, they form a united front against the malevolent forces of darkness. But as power attracts darkness, the villainous Veneria users seek to harness the necklaces' full potential for their dark ambitions. In this timeless battle between light and darkness, the fate of the world hangs in the balance.

CONTACTS

Instagram: jontheslayer202

Follow me on Instagram for updates, looks at my personal life and announcements. Feel free to send me a direct message—I'd love to hear from you!

TikTok: Jstackz_05

Find me on TikTok for engaging content related to my book. Join me for discussions, Q&A sessions, and fun videos about the world of my story and some other things I just do randomly. Don't forget to like, comment, and share!

Webnovel: JONXSLAYER

Dive deeper into the world of my book on Webnovel. Read exclusive chapters, interact with other readers, and stay up to date with the latest developments in the story. Your support means the world to me!

Thank you for your interest in my book. I appreciate your support and look forward to connecting with you on these platforms!

ABOUT THE AUTHOR

Jonathan Slater

Hello, my name is Jonathan Slater, and I'm thrilled to share a bit about myself with you. At 17 years old, I am a passionate writer who aspires to see my novels adapted into comics or animations in the future. It's my ultimate goal to bring my stories to life in visual mediums.

Currently, I'm attending college, pursuing a two-year sports coaching course. While my studies keep me busy, writing novels has always been my true passion. I dedicate my time to crafting engaging stories alongside my academic pursuits. I believe that this series holds the potential for great success and I'm excited to see where it takes me.

The inspiration behind my writing comes from my lifelong love for manga and anime. Over the years, these mediums have greatly influenced and fuelled my creativity. While I initially attempted drawing to create manga, it didn't quite work out as I had hoped. However, I found that writing allowed me to fully express my ideas and bring my stories to life in a way that suited me best. I'm also exploring future projects and hope to collaborate with an illustrator along the way.

As an author, I can't predict how long this journey will last, but I approach it with confidence and enthusiasm. I believe that with dedication and hard work, I can achieve great things in the world of storytelling.

Thank you for taking the time to read this. I sincerely appreciate your interest and support. Now that you know a bit more about me, I hope you'll join me on this exciting adventure as I continue to share my imagination through my novels.

KENZO

YOSHIDA

LEI

ALINA

Bonus Chapter: Kenzo

After the intense battles that shaped the fate of the Sasaki and Musenge Bloodlines, a new era of peace and harmony dawned upon the land. Kenzo, the last living descendant of the fabled Ogushi Clan, found himself facing a new chapter in his life.

With the war finally over, Kenzo returned to his village, Nuville, which had suffered greatly during the conflict. Determined to rebuild and heal the wounds of the past, Kenzo rallied the villagers and worked tirelessly to restore their homes and livelihoods.

With each passing day, the scars of war began to fade, replaced by the promise of a brighter future under Kenzo's guidance.

As the hero who had saved the Musenge Bloodline and brought an end to the tyranny of the Sasaki Empire, Kenzo found himself in a position of great influence. The people looked up to him as a leader, and the responsibility weighed heavily on his shoulders.

With the support of his fellow villagers and the Musenge Bloodline, Kenzo embraced his role as a symbol of hope and unity for the entire region.

Despite his newfound responsibilities, Kenzo never forgot his promise to Yoshida, the courageous warrior who had sacrificed himself to save the Musenge Bloodline. With deep reverence, Kenzo erected a memorial in Yoshida's honour, ensuring that his legacy would be forever remembered.

Driven by a desire to prevent future conflicts, Kenzo embarked on a journey to visit neighbouring bloodlines and forge alliances with people around the world. He sought to create a network of understanding and cooperation, with the hope of preventing bloodshed and fostering a lasting era of peace.

In the years that followed, Kenzo's efforts bore fruit. The Sasaki Empire, now under the leadership of Danzai, transformed into a beacon of reconciliation and prosperity. The bloodlines of the region began to coexist peacefully, united by the shared vision of a brighter future.

As the legend of Kenzo, the last of the Ogushi Clan, spread throughout the land, he became known not only for his prowess in battle but also for his unwavering commitment to peace.

Kenzo's journey was far from over, and the challenges ahead were as vast as the horizon. But guided by the spirit of Yoshida and the teachings of the Ogushi Clan, Kenzo walked forward with determination, striving to create a legacy of hope and harmony for generations to come.

And so, the tale of Kenzo, the last living descendant of the Ogushi Clan, continued as he embraced the destiny bestowed upon him, forever etching his name in the annals of history as a symbol of courage, resilience, and the power of unity.

Bonus Chapter: Yoshida

As the dust settled and the last echoes of the war faded away, Yoshida found himself in a realm unlike any he had ever known. He stood before a majestic gate adorned with ancient symbols, emanating a serene and ethereal glow. This was the entrance to the afterlife, a place where spirits transcended the boundaries of mortal existence.

Uncertain of what awaited him, Yoshida took a deep breath and stepped forward, the gate swinging open with otherworldly grace. As he entered, he felt a sense of peace and belonging enveloping him, as if he was finally coming home.

Before him stood the figures he had longed to see - Kenzo's parents, the revered leaders of the Ogushi Clan. Their presence was both awe-inspiring and comforting, their spirits imbued with a gentle warmth that instantly put Yoshida at ease.

"Welcome, Yoshida," Kenzo's father spoke, his voice carrying the weight of wisdom and kindness. "We have been waiting for you."

Yoshida bowed respectfully, feeling a mix of humility and gratitude in their presence. "Thank you for accepting me here, despite not being of your bloodline."

Kenzo's mother smiled tenderly, "Blood does not define family, Yoshida. You were a messenger of destiny, and your role in Kenzo's life was of utmost importance. We witnessed your bravery and loyalty, and for that, you are one of us."

With tears welling up in his eyes, Yoshida felt an overwhelming sense of belonging and acceptance. It was a feeling he had never experienced before, one that surpassed any earthly connection.

As they walked together, Kenzo's parents shared tales of their son's childhood, his journey of growth, and his unwavering determination to protect and bring harmony to the bloodlines. Yoshida, in turn, recounted the battles he had fought alongside Kenzo, the struggles they faced, and the ultimate triumph over evil.

They reached a tranquil garden, bathed in the soft glow of celestial light. There, Yoshida saw more figures - the ancestors of the Ogushi Clan, revered souls who had shaped their legacy for generations.

"I never thought I'd find myself among such esteemed company," Yoshida admitted, still in awe of the profound reunion.

"You earned your place here with your actions and heart," Kenzo's father said. "Your loyalty and dedication were integral to the restoration of the Ogushi Clan's legacy."

As they walked through the garden, Yoshida felt a deep connection with the spirits of the past. He exchanged stories with the ancestors, learning about their lives, their virtues, and the profound impact they had on their bloodline.

Among them, Yoshida found a mentor and guide - a wise and gentle spirit who had walked the path of a messenger long before him. This spirit shared invaluable wisdom with Yoshida, guiding him on the intricacies of his role in the afterlife.

Days turned to weeks, and time seemed to have a different rhythm in this ethereal realm. Yoshida's bond with Kenzo's parents and the spirits of the Ogushi Clan deepened, becoming a cherished connection that transcended time and space.

Yoshida knew that he could not return to the mortal world, but he found peace in knowing that he was now among those who had protected the land for generations. He embraced his role as a guardian spirit, watching over the bloodlines and offering guidance to those who sought to bring harmony and peace.

As the spirits of the Ogushi Clan flourished in the afterlife, Yoshida felt a sense of fulfilment like never before. His journey as a messenger had led him to a place of eternal purpose and love, where the bonds he forged in the mortal world only grew stronger with time.

In the realm beyond, Yoshida found a new home, united with the souls who had shaped the legacy of the Ogushi Clan, forever bound by a bond that transcended both time and death. His journey as a messenger, once a calling in the mortal world, now became an eternal commitment in the realm of spirits, where love, courage, and loyalty knew no boundaries.

Bonus Chapter: Lei Sasaki

In the depths of the Sasaki Empire, Lei's journey towards power began in betrayal and darkness. Born into the once-respected Sasaki Bloodline, Lei grew up in a world of privilege and entitlement. His father, the esteemed leader of the bloodline, had high hopes for his son, grooming him to one day take over the throne.

However, as Lei grew older, he harboured deep resentment towards his father's strict teachings and the weight of his legacy. The pressure to follow in his father's footsteps suffocated him, and he felt overshadowed by his father's achievements.

One fateful night, the weight of his emotions reached a boiling point. Enraged by his father's dismissive treatment during an argument, Lei's anger consumed him. Unable to control himself, he lashed out and struck his father with a fatal blow.

The reality of what he had done hit him like a tidal wave, and he stood in shock as his father's lifeless body lay before him. Panic and fear enveloped him, and in his desperation, he turned to his long-lived comrade, Alina.

Alina, cunning and ambitious, saw an opportunity in their father's death. Together, they consumed his blood, believing that it would grant them immense power and an unquenchable thirst for control.

United by their dark pact, Lei and Alina embarked on a path of vengeance and conquest. Driven by their thirst for power, they sought to annihilate the rival bloodlines that they perceived as threats to their dominance - the Ogushi and the Musenge.

Their reign of terror was ruthless, leaving a trail of destruction and despair in their wake. Lei revelled in his newfound strength, using his bloodline powers to manipulate and destroy those who dared to oppose him.

As the Sasaki Empire plunged into darkness under Lei's rule, he became a figure of fear and dread. His heart grew cold, and he lost touch with the humanity that once resided within him. Power became his sole purpose, and he stopped at nothing to achieve it.

The depths of his depravity knew no bounds, and he derived pleasure from the suffering he inflicted on others. He relished the chaos and cruelty, taking delight in the terror he instilled in his enemies.

Yet, even amidst his ruthless pursuit of power, a part of Lei still yearned for the validation and acceptance he had never received from his father. His insatiable thirst for control masked an underlying insecurity, a desperate need to prove himself worthy of his bloodline's name.

As he and Alina continued their conquest, Lei's thirst for vengeance expanded beyond the bloodlines. He sought to assert his dominance over anyone who dared to defy him, leaving a trail of devastation in his quest for absolute power.

The once-promising young boy had become a dark and twisted figure, consumed by ambition and darkness. The legacy of the Sasaki Bloodline had taken a sinister turn, and

Lei revelled in the malevolence that now defined him.

In the end, Lei's descent into darkness would lead him to a fateful encounter with the last living descendant of the Ogushi Clan, Kenzo. The clash of their bloodline energies marked the beginning of the final chapter in Lei's tumultuous journey, one that would determine the fate of the Sasaki Empire and its legacy.

Bonus Chapter: Danzai Musenge

long before the intense battles and the rise of the Musenge Bloodline, Danzai's journey began in a small and humble village nestled in the heart of the Musenge territory. He was born into a family with a rich history of warriors and protectors, known for their deep connection to the element of lightning.

From a young age, Danzai displayed extraordinary potential in harnessing the power of lightning. His family recognized his innate talent and knew that he was destined for greatness. They trained him rigorously, nurturing his abilities and instilling in him the values of honour, loyalty, and selflessness.

As he grew older, Danzai's reputation as a skilled and compassionate warrior spread throughout the village. He was admired not only for his exceptional combat skills but also for his unwavering dedication to the people he vowed to protect.

Danzai's leadership qualities emerged naturally, and he became a symbol of hope and strength for the villagers. When challenges arose, he was always the first to step forward, leading the charge to defend his people and uphold the honour of the Musenge Bloodline.

But life in the village was not always without trials. As a young man, Danzai faced a moment that would forever shape his destiny. An invading force from a neighbouring region threatened to bring destruction and chaos to his home.

Many lives were lost at the hands of the Sasaki Bloodline but not all perished in the Musenge Bloodline with only a remaining. Danzai was one of the survivors.

Danzai's journey was not without personal struggles and sacrifices. He faced moments of doubt and hardship, but each challenge only made him stronger and more resolute in his commitment to his people.

As the Musenge Bloodline found itself entangled in the tumultuous events of the main story, Danzai faced the ultimate test of his leadership. The battles and confrontations tested him physically and emotionally, but he never wavered in his pursuit of justice and peace for his people.

I am very proud of you my son. You're a light to others, they're always watching so make sure to guide them in the right direction. I am always here for you and I am here to believe in you and you should believe in yourself

Jonathan's Mother

Once Again, Thank You for Reading

Blanks

Printed in Great Britain
by Amazon